— SHAKESPEARE'S —

THE TEMPEST

Adapted by

Steve Barlow and Steve Skidmore

Illustrated by Edu Coll

W

FRANKLIN WATTS

LONDON • SYDNEY

FRANKLIN WATTS
FIRST PUBLISHED IN GREAT BRITAIN IN 2022
BY HODDER AND STOUGHTON

CREDITS:
EDITOR: GRACE GLENDINNING
DESIGNER: CATHRYN GILBERT
ILLUSTRATIONS: EDU COLL

PICTURE CREDITS: PAGE 109 COLIN WATERS / ALAMY STOCK PHOTO
EVERY ATTEMPT HAS BEEN MADE TO CLEAR COPYRIGHT. SHOULD
THERE BE ANY INADVERTENT OMISSION PLEASE APPLY TO THE
PUBLISHER FOR RECTIFICATION.

HB ISBN: 978 1 4451 8002 1
PB ISBN: 978 1 4451 8003 8

PRINTED IN CHINA

FRANKLIN WATTS
AN IMPRINT OF
HACHETTE CHILDREN'S GROUP
PART OF HODDER AND STOUGHTON
CARMELITE HOUSE
50 VICTORIA EMBANKMENT
LONDON EC4Y 0DZ

AN HACHETTE UK COMPANY
WWW.HACHETTE.CO.UK
WWW.HACHETTECHILDRENS.CO.UK

CONTENTS

William Shakespeare:

The Man, the Actor, the Author

William Shakespeare is considered to be one of the greatest writers who ever lived.

He was born in the market town of Stratford-upon-Avon in Warwickshire, England in 1564 and died there in 1616.

Shakespeare is usually referred to as an Elizabethan playwright but he actually lived during the reign of two monarchs: Elizabeth I and James I. When Elizabeth died in 1603, James, who was already King of Scotland, took over the English throne.

During Shakespeare's lifetime, he wrote nearly 40 plays and over 150 poems (mainly sonnets). He was also an actor, a very successful businessman and owned valuable buildings and land in London and Stratford.

His parents were John Shakespeare, a glove-maker and Stratford council official, and Mary Arden, who was the daughter of a wealthy local farmer. As the child of a reasonably well-off family, William attended the local grammar school, where he would have studied Latin and Greek as well as English literature and history.

In 1582, at the age of 18, he married Anne Hathaway. They had three children but by 1587, Shakespeare had left his wife and children in Stratford and moved to London. He joined an acting company and, by the early 1590s, was writing his own plays, becoming well known and successful in the world of London theatre.

Stratford-upon-Avon

London

In 1594, Shakespeare joined a new acting company, The Lord Chamberlain's Men, with his friend, the actor Richard Burbage. He would spend the rest of his life writing plays to be performed by this company and even became a part-owner of The Globe Theatre, which was built in 1599. The Lord Chamberlain's Men were so successful that when King James came to the throne, he became their sponsor and their name was changed to The King's Men.

From 1610, Shakespeare began to spend more time in Stratford. He died on 23rd April 1616. In the years following Shakespeare's death, two of his friends, John Heminge and Henry Condell, collected manuscripts and copies of his plays. They were printed in 1623 in an edition known as *The First Folio*. This collection of tragedies, comedies and historical plays helped to establish Shakespeare as a great playwright – possibly the greatest the world has ever known.

Another friend, the playwright Ben Jonson, said that Shakespeare's plays would prove to be "not of an age, but for all time".

Jonson was right. Shakespeare's plays have been translated into every major language and are performed across the world. They have also been turned into films, TV series, musicals, ballets and graphic novels!

The Tempest – The Play

The Tempest is thought to be the last play that William Shakespeare wrote on his own. It was first performed in 1611.

It is the story of Prospero, a magician who has been cast away on an island. By creating a storm (a tempest) Prospero manages to shipwreck his enemies on this island in order to take revenge for the crimes they committed against him when he was the Duke of Milan. The play was performed in front of King James I in 1611, and has continued to delight audiences with its mixture of magic, spirits, romance, monsters, music, dancing and slapstick comedy!

The Tempest is the only known Shakespearean play based wholly on an original story. Shakespeare usually "borrowed" ideas and storylines from other writers, but this seems to have been written without a previous source. It is a play of memorable characters and famous quotations ...

"Misery acquaints a man with strange bedfellows."

Trinculo Act 2 Scene 2

"Thought is free."

Stephano Act 3 Scene 2

"Now I will believe that there are unicorns ..."

Sebastian Act 3 Scene 3

"We are such stuff
As dreams are made on,
and our little life
Is rounded with a sleep."

Prospero Act 4 Scene 1

"Be not afeard. The isle is full of noises, sounds, and sweet airs that give delight and hurt not."

Caliban Act 3 Scene 2

"O brave new world
That has such people in't."

Miranda Act 5 Scene 1

With its universal themes of love, betrayal, revenge, forgiveness and magic, it is easy to see why *The Tempest* is considered to be one of Shakespeare's greatest and most beloved plays.

THE TEMPEST

THE MEDITERRANEAN SEA
SIXTEENTH CENTURY

THE KING OF NAPLES AND HIS SON, FERDINAND, ARE SAILING HOME FROM TUNIS IN NORTH AFRICA, WHERE THEY HAVE BEEN ATTENDING THE WEDDING OF THE KING'S DAUGHTER.

ALSO ON BOARD THE KING'S SHIP IS ANTONIO, DUKE OF MILAN, WHO STOLE THE TITLE FROM HIS BROTHER, PROSPERO, TWELVE YEARS AGO.

A TEMPEST (STORM) SUDDENLY BREAKS OUT, TOSSING THE SHIP ON THE RAGING SEAS. LITTLE DO THE ROYAL PARTY KNOW THAT THIS IS THE WORK OF PROSPERO, WHO WAITS ON A NEARBY ISLAND, READY TO TAKE HIS REVENGE...

Milan

ITALY

Naples

NORTH AFRICA

List of Main Characters

Dramatis Personae

PROSPERO

Magician and formerly the
Duke of Milan, now lives
on a magical island

MIRANDA

Prospero's daughter
who lives on the island
with him

CALIBAN

A monster who has lived
on the island his whole
life, son of the witch,
Sycorax, and a demon

ARIEL

A spirit of the air
who is serving Prospero in
return for him freeing them
from Sycorax's magical prison

ALONSO

King of Naples

SPIRITS OF THE ISLES

Ruled by Prospero and led by Ariel

FERDINAND

Alonso's son and
Prince of Naples

SEBASTIAN

Brother of Alonso,
King of Naples

ANTONIO

Prospero's brother and
now the Duke of Milan

GONZALO

An honest advisor
to King Alonso

STEPHANO

A drunken and
rude butler

TRINCULO

A court jester and
friend of Stephano

BOSUN

Officer in charge of
keeping the sailors on
King Alonso's ship in order

ADRIAN

A Lord

MASTER

Captain of
King Alonso's ship

FRANCISCO

A Lord

ACT 1

ON PROSPERO'S ISLAND IN
THE MEDITERRANEAN SEA

ANTONIO
ALONSO
SEBASTIAN
GONZALO

STEPHANO

TRINCULO

FERDINAND

And what about the King's **ship** and the **sailors** on it?

It is in a hidden bay and the sailors are all asleep.

The **rest** of the fleet is heading back to Naples. They think they saw the King's ship sink and believe that that everyone on board is **dead**.

If you complain to me **again**, I'll imprison you in a tree for **another** twelve years!

Please forgive me, Master. I will **never** complain again.

Good!

Now **do what I ask**, and I will give you your freedom within **two days**!

Tell me what to do!

Turn yourself into a water fairy. Then become **invisible** to everyone but **me**.

That's good. **Now**, this is what I want you to do ...

33

41

44

45

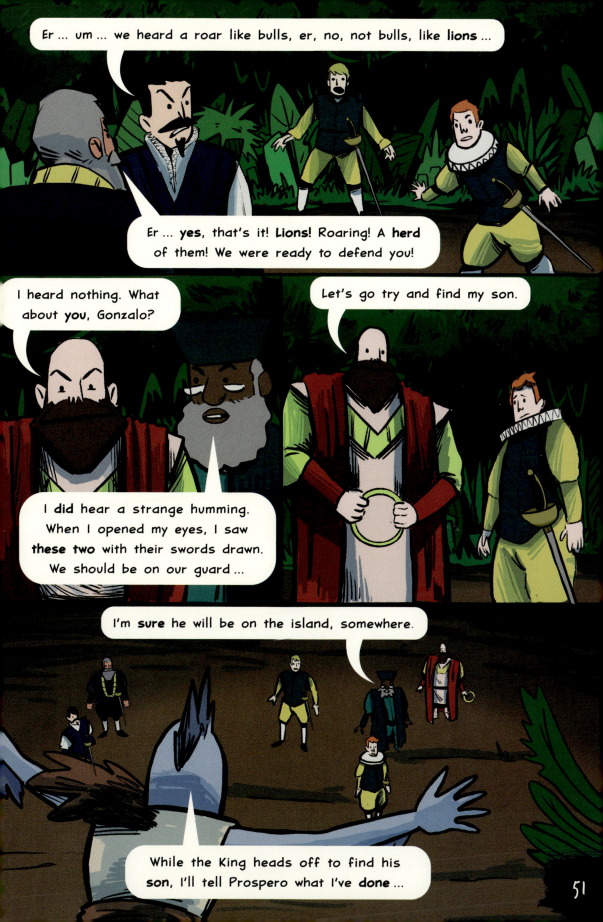

51

57

ACT 3

MEANWHILE, FERDINAND HAS BEEN PUT TO WORK BY PROSPERO!

She's **ten times** gentler than her father! Thinking of her makes this task **easy**!

Although this work is hard and I am a prince, I'm doing it for the woman I **love**!

My father is in his study. He won't be around for another three hours.

Don't **work** so hard! You can rest.

I **need** to finish this task.

I'll help.

No, you are too **precious** to me to do that!

If **you** can do it, so can I!

61

But this violent magic is **wrong**! I will do it **no more**, except to cast one **final** spell.

And afterwards, I will **break** my staff ...

... and **throw** my books into the deepest sea!

But before I do this ...

83

88

I invite you **all** to stay here tonight, and I will tell you my story ...

I look forward to hearing it.

Then **tomorrow** we can sail back to Naples ... Miranda and Ferdinand will be married ...

... and I will then return to Milan, where I will spend the rest of my days.

But **first** there is something I have to do.

Ariel! Follow me.

ARIEL, I
RELEASE YOU TO
THE ELEMENTS!

You are
free ...

Farewell, my sweet spirit!

Storytelling in The Tempest

The action of *The Tempest* takes place in one day. The events of the previous twelve years, leading up to this day, are told in a series of speeches by Prospero.

In **ACT 1**, the action and themes are set up very quickly. It starts dramatically as Prospero creates the tempest that brings his enemies to the island. We learn the history of his thirst for revenge; we meet the fascinating and unusual Ariel and Caliban; and indeed Ferdinand and Miranda fall in love, all in a 'storm' of action to get the play started.

ACT 2 is another busy act, with each role in the grand story being filled. The royal party is introduced and we quickly realise who is "good" and who is "bad": Gonzalo is kind and tries to cheer up Alonso, while Sebastian and Antonio are the play's scheming villains. There is slapstick humour, drunken, bawdy dialogue and singing, with Trinculo and Stephano providing a comical contrast to the treachery.

ACT 3 is one of spectacle and drama: romance, magic, comedy, music and murder-plotting. It is a dramatic act in which drunkenness, proposals, feasts and temptations are all controlled and directed by Prospero and his magic. His plan is in full swing, and Ariel is clearly crucial to its success.

ACT 4 sees Prospero bringing his plans to fruition. He gives his permission for Miranda and Ferdinand to marry and celebrates with grand, magical entertainment. Prospero and Ariel deal with Caliban, Trinculo and Stephano by having them chased off by demons.

In **ACT 5**, all is explained to the various characters who still find themselves puzzled by their situation. Promises are fulfilled, apologies made, forgiveness bestowed, plotters put to work, freedom granted. Prospero promises to tell the whole story before setting off to Milan the next day on the King's ship and we are left with the sense that, "they all lived happily ever after"!

Bonus! Epilogue

In a final soliloquy, Prospero gives up his magic, and the actor playing him "breaks the fourth wall" by stepping out of the role he has been playing and asks for the audience's applause.

Themes in The Tempest

The Tempest has been a source of inspiration for artists, poets and composers for over four hundred years. The play even helped to shape and inspire the opening ceremonies of the 2012 Olympic and Paralympic Games held in London. The words *Be not afeard; the isle is full of noises* were engraved on a 23-tonne bell that was sounded during the Olympic opening ceremony.

Magic

The Tempest is a play full of magic. In Shakespeare's time, many people believed in magic and witchcraft. In fact, King James I had a fascination with the subject.

Prospero controls most of the magical action in the play, but he uses his magic for good, unlike Calban's mother, the witch Sycorax, who used her powers for evil (see page 30).

From the beginning of the play, when Prospero creates the tempest, to the final scene, when he has his enemies in his power, Prospero uses his magic to control and direct the actions of the characters (just as a playwright controls what will happen in the play).

In the end, Prospero gives up his books and his staff, knowing that he does not need his magical powers anymore.

Exploration and Colonisation

The idea of European nations taking over lands inhabited by people they called "savages" and forcing their culture on these people was an important subject in Shakespeare's day. European explorers told stories of "exotic" far-away lands they had "discovered".

At this point in history, explorers including Sir Walter Raleigh were in the thick of setting up colonies in places such as the "New World" of America.

This certainly affected Shakespeare in his writing of *The Tempest*. Caliban can be seen to represent the native peoples who were forced into becoming "civilised" by these colonial powers, who are represented by Prospero. To the modern reader, Caliban can be seen as a more complex and sympathetic character than he would have been by many viewers of Shakespeare's time.

Betrayal and Forgiveness

There is a lot of betrayal and treachery in *The Tempest* with Prospero suffering a great deal! He is betrayed by his brother, Antonio (aided by Sebastian and Alonso), and also Caliban, who plots with Stephano and Trinculo to kill him.

However, Prospero does not kill any of those that did him wrong, even though he has total power over them.

This forgiveness of his enemies is in direct contrast to the actions shown in many plays of the period, where characters do not forgive, but instead take revenge in nasty and horrible ways! Although Prospero feels that he has good reason to exact revenge, Ariel persuades him not to, saying that he should show mercy instead. Prospero agrees, saying that it is better to forgive than to take revenge.

Caliban also feels betrayed by Prospero, claiming that he was kind to Prospero and Miranda when they first arrived, only to be forced into becoming Prospero's servant (see page 35).

Imprisonment and Freedom

All the characters in *The Tempest* are trapped or imprisoned at some point and want to be free of their situation.

Prospero wants to be free from the island, Caliban and Ariel want to be free from Prospero's rule and the king's party are trapped by Prospero's magic.

Storm and Calm

In Shakespeare's day, it was thought that there was a link between important events and the weather. Bad weather signalled a great disturbance in human affairs, while fine, calm weather was seen as a good omen.

Prospero's magic causes his moods to be reflected in the weather of the magic isle. When he is angry, he can raise a storm to "wreck" Alonso's ship and bring Ferdinand to the island, or thunder and lightning to terrify the royal party when Ariel appears to them as a monster. Thunder follows Caliban around when he is out of favour.

When Prospero is calm, the weather settles – the magical "voices" of the isle can be heard. At length, Prospero draws his enemies into a circle to the sounds of solemn music, and peace descends.

Work and Idleness

Antonio and Sebastian, having stolen Prospero's dukedom, now threaten to steal Alonso's throne. Stephano and Trinculo involve Caliban in their drunken idleness. Caliban works for Prospero unwillingly, with many complaints, while Ariel, even while desiring his freedom, does so willingly. Ferdinand, who carries out Prospero's wishes by carrying logs around (a very unaristocratic chore!) through his own choice, proves that he is worthy to marry Miranda. Throughout the play, honest work and obedience are portrayed as more likely to lead to rewards than complaint or plotting.

Shakespeare's Language

Inventions

Shakespeare used more than 20,000 different words in his plays and poems. Around 1,700 of these were new or were the first recorded use of the word! He invented new words and phrases by making them up or by putting two words together to make a new one, or adding or subtracting parts of words.

Poetry

Shakespeare's works were often written in a mixture of verse and prose (normal speech). Important and high-ranking characters (kings, lords, etc.) usually speak in verse. Prose is more likely to be spoken by servants.

There are two main types of poetry in Shakespeare's plays:

Blank verse

Rhyming poetry

In *The Tempest*, Shakespeare mainly uses blank verse.

Blank Verse

This is a type of poetry that follows these rules:

Each line has 10 or 11 syllables.

Each line has five strong beats.

Think of a heart beating: de **DUM** de **DUM** de **DUM** de **DUM** de **DUM**. This is similar to how the beat or stress falls on the syllables in the verse. See how this works in the line to follow. When you say the line, you place the emphasis on the word in bold.

De - **Dum** - de - **Dum** - de - **Dum** - de - **Dum** - de - **Dum**

Ye - **elves** - of - **hills.** - brooks - **stand** - ing - **lakes** - and - **groves.**

A Soliloquy

This is a speech spoken by one character; we're listening to their thoughts. They are thinking out loud to themselves, or speaking directly to the audience, not to another character. (In the graphic novel, we have put some of these in "thought bubbles".)

Caliban and Ferdinand both have soliloquies in the play (see pages 52 and 58 of the graphic novel).

Puns and Word Play

Shakespeare uses puns and word play throughout *The Tempest*.

The comedy scenes involving Trinculo, Stephano and Caliban and the speeches between Antonio and Sebastian are full of these devices:

Adrian:	The air breathes upon us here most sweetly.
Sebastian:	As if it had lungs, and rotten ones.
Antonio:	Or, as 'twere perfumed by a fen.* (see page 43)

Shakespeare's audience would have loved these type of jokes – there are a lot of rude ones as well!

Songs

Of all Shakespeare's plays, *The Tempest* has the most music in it. Characters speak of hearing music and Caliban's famous speech tells us that the island is:

"full of noises, sounds and sweet airs,

that give delight and hurt not." (see page 63)

The songs range from the bawdy, drunken singing of Stephano and Trinculo to the beautiful, operatic, formal arias sung by Ariel.

The Tempest also contains a masque. Masques were pageants with music and were a popular form of entertainment among the wealthier classes of the period. The masque occurs in the play when Prospero introduces the spirits of the isles to Ferdinand and Miranda, to bless them (see page 71).

*a swamp

Fun Facts

Miranda is really a boy!

In Shakespeare's day only males could act on the stage. So all the female parts were actually played by males! Several of Shakespeare's plays also have female characters pretending to be male, including *Twelfth Night*, *As You Like It* and *The Merchant of Venice*. So, when you watched one of these plays you were watching a boy pretending to be a girl pretending to be a boy!

A Real-life Prospero

Shakespeare might have based the character of Prospero on a real person.

Dr John Dee was a scientist and mathematician who was the court astronomer to Queen Elizabeth I. However, he was also regarded as a *magus* – someone who had interests in subjects that were regarded as "supernatural", such as alchemy, astrology and the occult. He was also known to own a huge library of books, just as Prospero had when he was Duke of Milan.

Line up!

There are 2,039 lines of text in The Tempest, making it Shakespeare's second-shortest play. Only *The Comedy of Errors* has fewer lines.

Prospero speaks nearly a third of all the lines in the play.

Sci-Fi

The Tempest was the basis for the 1956 sci-fi film, *Forbidden Planet.*

Instead of being set on Prospero's island, the action takes place on a planet, Altair IV.

The main characters are called Professor Morbius and Altaira (Prospero and Miranda). Ariel is not a magical spirit but a robot called Robby! The character of Robby the Robot was a massive hit with audiences, and later appeared in many movies and comic books.

Publication

Shakespeare's plays weren't printed or even written up as complete plays before they were first performed. Each actor was given his part on a scroll. They had to learn their lines from this.

The "platt" or plot of the play was a list of the scenes with the exits and entrances. This was posted backstage for the actors to follow.

The Tempest first appeared in print as part of the *First Folio* in 1623, where 36 of Shakespeare's plays were published together for the first time. It is the very first play printed in the book, leading people to think it was the first play that Shakespeare wrote, rather than it actually being the last he completed on his own.

Book Fact

There were three main sizes of books in Shakespeare's time.

Folio

A book made from sheets of paper that are folded once to make four pages from one sheet.

Quarto

A smaller book. The sheets of paper are folded twice to make eight pages from one sheet.

Octavo

An even smaller book! The sheets of paper are folded four times to make 16 pages from one sheet.

Performing The Play!

In Shakespeare's time, drama performance and theatre spaces were developing in various ways across the globe. England was no exception.

When Shakespeare began his acting career, there were very few theatres in London.

Plays were performed in inn yards and in the halls and houses of the monarch or the wealthy. But, by the end of Shakespeare's life, plays were being performed in purpose-built theatres across London, where performances took place every day (except Sundays), all year round.

The first purpose-built London playhouse appeared in 1576 when James Burbage, father of Shakespeare's friend, Richard Burbage, constructed a building for performing plays. He called it The Theatre! The success of this space led to other playhouses being built across London.

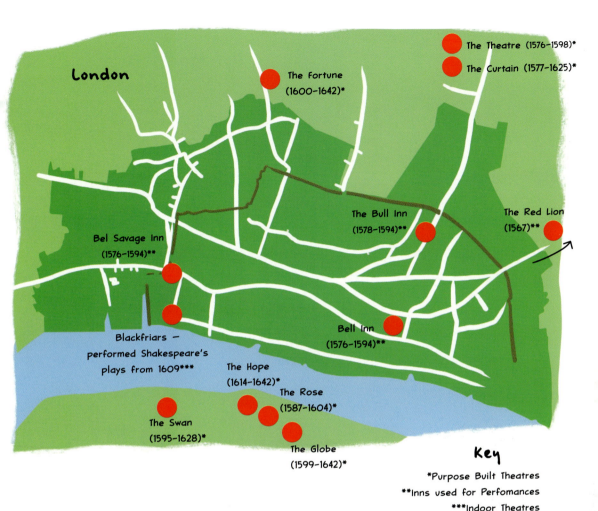

London

The Theatre (1576–1598)*

The Curtain (1577–1625)*

The Fortune (1600–1642)*

The Bull Inn (1578–1594)**

The Red Lion (1567)**

Bel Savage Inn (1576–1594)**

Bell Inn (1576–1594)**

Blackfriars — performed Shakespeare's plays from 1609***

The Hope (1614–1642)*

The Rose (1587–1604)*

The Swan (1595–1628)*

The Globe (1599–1642)*

Key
*Purpose Built Theatres
**Inns used for Perfomances
***Indoor Theatres

Deadly Serious Fact

Bubonic plague, or the Black Death, was a big part of Shakespeare's world. Thousands of people died from the plague across the globe.

It is thought to have been passed on by rat fleas, which carried deadly bacteria. If you caught the plague, there was a fifty-fifty chance of survival. Whenever there was an outbreak in London, the theatres were shut down, which meant no money for playwrights or actors.

The Theatre

A trip to the theatre to see a play in Shakespeare's time was very different from today. People didn't sit still. They stood, walked around, shouted and chatted to each other. The audience could buy ale, wine, pies, fruit, tobacco and nuts, all while the play was being performed. The audience got as close to the action as possible, so they could hear the actors – there were no microphones in Shakespeare's day!

The plays were aimed at all levels of society – from Lords and Ladies of the court down to tradespeople and commoners. Criminals also visited the playhouses, ready to pick the pockets of unsuspecting members of the audience.

Depending on how rich (and important) you were, you could choose where to sit.

In 1594, a worker's pay was about 8 pence a day, so it meant that plays were affordable to a lot of London's population and therefore many people went to the theatre. The large theatres, such as The Globe, could hold up to 3,000 spectators, including 1,000 groundlings (see opposite).

For indoor playhouses, it was more expensive and therefore the audience members were wealthier.

The Globe Theatre was built in 1599.

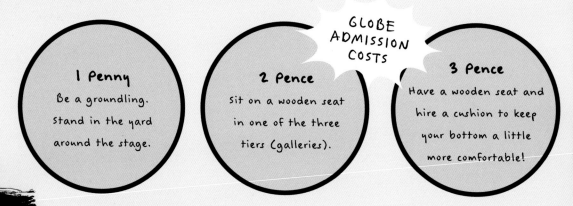

GLOBE ADMISSION COSTS

1 Penny
Be a groundling. Stand in the yard around the stage.

2 Pence
Sit on a wooden seat in one of the three tiers (galleries).

3 Pence
Have a wooden seat and hire a cushion to keep your bottom a little more comfortable!

The Globe Theatre

Open-air playhouse

There would be a different show every afternoon. Coloured flags were used to advertise what play was being put on that day.

Red – History
Black – Tragedy
White – Comedy

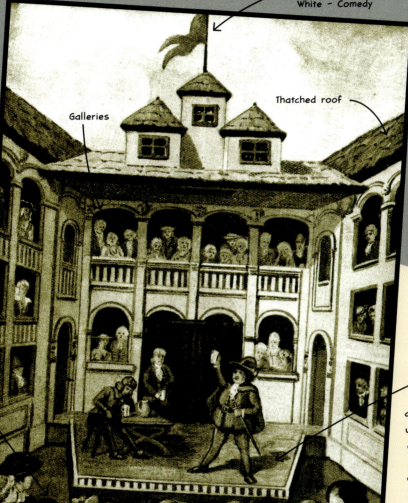

Galleries

Thatched roof

Standing area groundlings

Stage
(Under stage and above stage used for special effects, storing costumes and changing rooms for actors)

6 Pence
Sit in the Lord's Gallery – rooms on either side of the balcony at the back of the stage.

12 Pence
(1 shilling)
Sit on the stage.

30 Pence
(2 shillings & 6 pence – or half a crown)
you could sit in a private box.

Glossary

The World of Shakespeare's Words

Early Modern English Language was only about 100 years old when Shakespeare started writing in the sixteenth century. Because he often wrote in verse, in order to fit the words into the necessary rhythm, some of the sentence order seems odd to us today.

As Shakespeare was writing over 400 years ago, some of the words and phrases he uses can look a bit strange. Some are so old, that we don't use them any more!

Thou, thee, thy and thine

Shakespeare uses these words A LOT. But they aren't as confusing as they seem!

thou	means	you
thee	means	you
thy	means	your
thine	means	your

Sometimes two words are put together. Watch out for the apostrophe!

'twas	means	it was
'twere	means	it were
'tis	means	it is
is't	means	is it

Sometimes words have extra letters. Take off the **t** or **st** and see what's left!

hast	means	has
wilt	means	will
dost	means	does
thinkst	means	think
hath	means	has
didst	means	did

Some more old words:

art	means	are
ere	means	before
forfeit	means	penalty
forsaken	means	abandoned
hence	means	from here
hie	means	go (hurry)
wherefore	means	why
ye	means	you
yonder	means	there
fie!	means	an exclamation of disapproval

Shakespeare Timeline

We often have no clear information about the dates of Shakespeare's plays. Scholars who study Shakespeare have to rely on information such as the way each play is put together, the language Shakespeare uses and details in the text that connect to parts of history.

Therefore, the dates of the plays given below are "best guesses" as to the years in which they were written and first performed.

1558   Queen Mary I dies and her sister, Queen Elizabeth I, takes the throne of England.

1564   Shakespeare is born. Horse-drawn coaches first appear in England.

1567   The first purpose-built theatre in England is built – The Red Lion in Stepney, London.

1576   The Theatre is built in London by James Burbage. 180,000 people now live in London. 300,000 live in Paris, France.

1582   Shakespeare marries Anne Hathaway.

1582   The theatres close down in London due to an outbreak of plague. Thousands of people die.

London's first waterworks is founded.

1583   Susanna (Shakespeare's daughter) is born. (See also 1585)

1584   Ivan The Terrible, first ruler of Russia, dies.

1585   Hamnet and Judith (twins – Shakespeare's son and daughter) are born.

1587   Shakespeare leaves Stratford-upon-Avon and his family for London.

The Rose Theatre is built in London by Philip Henslowe (on Bankside).

Mary Queen of Scots is executed.

1588   The Spanish Armada invade England, but are defeated.

1590/1   Shakespeare's first plays, **THE TWO GENTLEMAN OF VERONA** and **THE TAMING OF THE SHREW**, are performed.

1591   Shakespeare dedicates his poem, *Venus and Adonis*, to the Earl of Southampton. This poem earns him a lot of money!

Tea is first drunk in England.

1592   Shakespeare is mentioned in the press as an up-and-coming playwright.

Plague! All London playhouses are closed for two years.

Many of the acting companies tour the country.

Shakespeare begins writing poems.

The Imjin Wars between Japan and Korea begin.

1593   Playwright and friend of Shakespeare, Christopher Marlowe, is killed in a brawl.

1594   Shakespeare's poem, *The Rape of Lucrece*, is published. Again, it is dedicated to the Earl of Southampton.

1595   Shakespeare becomes a shareholder in The Lord Chamberlain's Men (a very successful and popular acting company).

ROMEO AND JULIET

1596	Shakespeare's son, Hamnet, dies. Shakespeare's father, John, is granted a coat of arms.
	England sees its first tomatoes – and its first flushing toilet.
	A MIDSUMMER NIGHT'S DREAM
1597	Shakespeare buys New Place in Stratford – one of the largest houses in the town.
	Transportation to English colonies is first used as a punishment for criminals.
1598	**MUCH ADO ABOUT NOTHING**
1599	The Globe Theatre is built.
1601	**HAMLET**
	Shakespeare's father dies.
1603	Queen Elizabeth dies.
	James VI of Scotland takes the throne with the title James I.
	Plague hits London. Over 30,000 people die. The theatres are closed again.
	The Lord Chamberlain's Men change their name to The King's Men.
	They perform at the King's courts and are recognised as the leading theatre company of the time.
1604	The Globe reopens.
1605	The Gunpowder Plot fails to blow up King James and his ministers.
	In Spain, Cervantes publishes Part 1 of the world's first novel, *Don Quixote*.
1606	**MACBETH**
	Theatres are ordered to close if the weekly number of people who die from the plague rises above 30. Theatres closed July – December.
1607	Shakespeare's daughter Susanna marries John Hall, a physician in Stratford.

	Shakespeare's brother, Edmund (an actor), dies.
	Founding of Jamestown, Virginia – first English colony in North America.
1608	Shakespeare's mother, Mary, dies.
	Shakespeare becomes a grandfather! Elizabeth is born to Susanna and John Hall.
	The King's Men begin to perform at an indoor theatre at Blackfriars.
	The telescope is invented by a Dutch scientist and used by Galileo.
1609	Shakespeare's *Sonnets* are published.
	The Blue Mosque is built in Constantinople (now Istanbul).
1610	Shakespeare spends more time in Stratford.
1611	**THE TEMPEST**
1612	Shakespeare's brother, Gilbert, dies.
	The decimal point is first used by German mathematician Pitiscus.
	The Dutch establish a trading post on Manhattan Island (later New York).
1613	The Globe Theatre burns down during a performance of Henry VIII.
	Shakespeare buys a house in Blackfriars, London.
1614	The Globe Theatre is rebuilt.
1616	Shakespeare's daughter, Judith, marries Thomas Quiney, a Stratford wine merchant.
	Shakespeare dies.
1623	Shakespeare's plays are published. The *First Folio* contains 36 of his plays.